The Silver
Stallion

Cover illustration by **Roger Payne**

Inside the book . . .

Janet Wickham illustrated "The Silver Stallion" and "Who's Boss?"

Jane Ettridge illustrated "Two for One", "Off to a Bumpy Start", "Save Our Stables" and "For the Best".

Francis Phillipps illustrated "A Bit Special", "A Taste for Excitement", "Standards" and "Happy-Go-Unlucky".

Gavin Rowe illustrated "Never Again".

AWARD PONY STORIES

The Silver Stallion

...and other pony stories

ROSEMARY SIMMONDS

AWARD PUBLICATIONS

ISBN 0-86163-312-1

Text copyright © 1989 Award Publications Limited

First published 1989
Published by Award Publications Limited,
Spring House, Spring Place
Kentish Town, London NW5 3BH

Printed in Hungary

CONTENTS

There it was! The wonderful silver stallion!

The Silver Stallion

Lauren's legs dropped to fit snugly behind the pommel arch and her feet wedged into the broad, wooden stirrups as she let her hips follow the lurching movement of the saddle. Her Quarter Horse, Lightning Tree, slipped and skidded his way down the steep slope. When the pines parted, Lauren touched her heels to Lightning's sides; he sprang onto the clear ground and stepped straight into a smooth lope.

"Good boy!" Lauren patted his neck. Poor Lightning was a good horse but

7

just a shade too slow off the starting block. Lauren did not appreciate him as much as he deserved.

It was only ten days to the rodeo in Tappo, down on the plain and Lauren needed to put in some practice or she would lose the calf-roping again. Lauren loved the ranch, with its hidden valley high in the mountains, but right now she would give anything to be on a cattle station. How could she possibly win when all she had to practise upon were fence posts and sheep. Lauren brought her horse to a standstill and singled out a tubby lamb. She put her heels to Lightning's sides, while at the same time checking him with the rein. The horse began to jump on the spot.

"Three, two, one," Lauren counted aloud ... "Go!"

Lightning bounced, taking two strides before he was away. "Why must you do that?" Lauren complained, but by then all her attention was focused on cutting out the lamb.

The Silver Stallion

Lauren kept her eyes on the lamb

"You are supposed to be fast on the draw, Lightning," Lauren reminded her horse as they walked back down the valley. "I wish you'd quit the dancing around and leap away at a gallop like you are supposed to." Despite her severe tone she found it difficult to be cross with Lightning for long, he was too good a friend. Lightning had been promised to her before he was born, as his foaling was due on her birthday. She could still remember the private wish she had kept that he would be pure white. The chances were a million to one off brown stock, but Lauren had a passion for Albinos. The colt turned out to be a bay with a jagged stripe along his nose. Lauren called him Lightning Tree.

Once home, Lauren turned Lightning into the corral and waited as she always did for his habitual roll. First he would scrape up the earth, then pad out a circle; the forelegs would buckle, then the hind legs and over he would go.

Maybe she walked back more quietly than usual. Maybe her parents were talking so intently they did not hear her step. At any rate, Lauren was sure the words she overheard were never meant to reach her ears.

"No Dave," she heard her mother's

voice. "You can't sell the brood mares, not after all the work you've put in. I know how much they mean to you."

"What else can I do?" asked her father. "I can hardly ask the boys to go another month on half-pay."

"I know . . . but . . . Oh, how come it's got so bad, Dave?" cried her mother.

"Lots of things," Lauren heard her father explain. "Business is slack in the timber yard just now and then there's the new barn we put up last autumn. Also, the sheep haven't recovered from that fluke attack. If we had got a really good colt out of those mares it would have helped, but Little Boss doesn't seem able to produce them any more."

"Maybe you should invest in a new stallion," suggested her mother.

"Myra! I am telling you our debts are outgrowing The Rockies and you advise me to buy a new stallion!" exploded Lauren's father.

Lauren hurried away, shutting her ears. She went up to her room and

opened the window wide. Her father in debt! It was hard to believe. Did Kelly know? Lauren thought of her older sister, last seen practising waist bends to a Michael Jackson cassette. No, Kelly wouldn't guess *that* unless her parents wrote the awful news on their foreheads.

On Tuesday they had a caller. He arrived in a white Mercedes. Lauren took in the cream suit and the glowing cheeks and decided she didn't like him. "Kelly, fix the dinner tonight, would

13

you?" asked her father. "Lauren, run along and feed the horses."

"It's only five, they aren't usually fed until six," Lauren complained. Lauren was sure this man had something to do with the debts and she wanted to stay.

"It won't hurt for them to have it early," insisted her father.

Lauren sped round the feed room, searching for an excuse to go back inside. The old mare, Tammy, called to her. She was due to foal any day. Lauren dropped the scoop and ran indoors. Her mother looked white. Her father had a cigarette in his fingers, though he was supposed to have given up smoking. "What should I feed Tammy?" asked Lauren and her father replied: "Leave her, I'll see to her when I'm finished."

"But she'll fret if the others are fed and not her," persisted Lauren, crossing the room to get a better look at the plan their visitor had laid out on the table. "What is it?" Lauren asked, then her eyes widened and her heart

"That looks like our house!"

missed a beat. "That looks like our house!"

"And so it is, little lady," crooned their visitor, Mr. Fleming. "I was just showing your Pa what a wonderful idea it would be to build an activity resort here. This lovely old house would make an authentic club and the outbuildings would be apartments." He pointed to a concrete block. "People would come here for skiing, fishing and to ride horses up the mountains to log cabins. Do you think folks would enjoy doing that?"

"You want to build it here?" asked Lauren in surprise. Mr. Fleming directed his answer to Lauren's father. "It's a prime site. Our company would consider it a valuable acquisition." Lauren saw the cigarette tremble between her father's fingers and remembered the debts he had talked of. A sale to Mr. Fleming would pay them all off.

"Do you have to sell?" Lauren asked her father when he joined her in the

yard later. "We owe a lot of money, Lauren and the bank won't wait for ever," he sighed.

"But this is our home!" exclaimed Lauren. "Couldn't you sell that bit of forest up by Bright Creek instead? No-one ever goes there."

"Bright Creek?" He shook his head. "I couldn't sell that. Did you know there used to be Indians up there, Lauren. They had a herd of white horses ... unusual for Indians. They generally like painted horses," he smiled. "Bright Creek is a special place

17

because I met your mother there."

Special! Lauren punched a fist into the bed later that night. Pa was crazy not to sell Bright Creek instead. She would go up there tomorrow and look the place over. It sounded just right for Mr. Fleming and he would love the story of an Indian encampment.

There were jobs to do about the house next day so Lauren did not get away until the afternoon. She cantered Lightning across the upper valley, then struck out along the eastern trail covering the ground at a good pace until she turned onto the old track for Bright Creek. The grass was waist high. More than once Lauren had to dismount to lead Lightning round a fallen tree. Bright Creek hadn't been visited in years.

At last she heard the river chuckling in the distance. "I guess you'd like a drink, wouldn't you?" she said to her horse. Lightning ignored her. "Hey, what is it?" His neck was rigid beneath her hand and his whole body had

More than once Lauren had to dismount

started to tremble. Lauren followed the line of his pricked ears to the opposite slope. The trees hissed as something moved through them. Lauren's stomach dropped into her boots. A mountain lion!

Silver-white flashed between the trees. Lauren shaded her eyes with her hand, straining to see. The creature was big, as big as Lightning and moving up the slope away from them. It reached the skyline and stopped, looking back at them. Lauren gasped, her mouth falling open.

Standing on the brow was a huge Albino stallion.

"Oh my!" Lauren breathed. Lightning backed, reluctant to go down the steep slope. "Come on!" Lauren urged. "We've got to get closer."

Lightning took the descent slowly, bracing himself as the scree carried him down. Lauren caught hold of the pommel as he waded through the small river then launched himself at the opposite bank. By the time they had

scrambled to the top, the Albino had gone. Lauren leaned out of the saddle and then dismounted to look for his tracks. The grass was straight. The earth smooth and firm, except for the places where Lightning had stamped upon it. "Where has he gone?" Lauren muttered, remounting and standing in her stirrups to scan the horizon. Trees rippled and a deer bounded away, but otherwise there was nothing.

"He can't have just vanished!" Lauren exclaimed to herself. "He's got to be here somewhere." Refusing to give up, she rode Lightning further up the head of the valley to a clearing where the stream cascaded over bare rock.

Lauren's brow wrinkled. A horse like that must have a herd. If not, he would have been challenging their own Little Boss for his mares by now. So where had he come from? She touched the reins to Lightning's neck and set him westward for home. A colt as good looking as that couldn't just get lost. He was of a type to be noticed. But what if he had been born in the wild . . . what if no one laid claim to him . . .

Lauren's mind began to race. Albino's were valuable, especially pure white ones like that stallion. They had a habit of imprinting their colour upon their offspring. Hadn't her mother said they should get a new stallion!

Lauren looked over her shoulder as they passed out of Bright Creek valley. If she could catch him, the silver stallion would solve their problems.

With a horse like that to breed from, her father would never sell the ranch.

Lauren turned Lightning loose, then ran to the house. "Where's Pa?" she asked as she stepped into the kitchen.

"He's gone over to the timber yard," her mother told her. "What's up? Is it Tammy?"

"I've found a wild horse," she announced. "An Albino stallion! Ma, he's fantastic!" Mrs. Berger continued to roll pastry for a blueberry pie. "A wild horse, huh?" she murmured.

"I saw him, all right!" insisted Lauren.

"Honey, there are no wild horses left in these mountains, you know that," said her mother.

"I did see him!" Lauren repeated and ran back outside to Lightning, who never contradicted her. "I'll prove it to them," she vowed. "When we catch that stallion they'll know it's true."

Lauren spent the rest of the week practising with the lasso and told everyone that she was training for the coming rodeo. By the end of the week, Lightning had got the hang of it and she had progressed from roping fence posts to catching Rusty, one of the older stock-horses.

On Friday afternoon, Lauren rode back to Bright Creek. A hawk drifted above her on silent wings. With each gust of the breeze the pine trees shivered, but otherwise nothing moved. Lauren felt the excitement seep out of her. Finding a needle in a haystack would be child's play compared to this.

Most of the day was spent practising with the lasso

She turned her horse up the valley to the pool beneath the cascade and dismounted. Lightning took two strides into the water and began to drink. Lauren crouched at the edge and splashed her arms and face to cool off. Her fingers played with the stones as she made her plans. One pebble glittered dully in the water. Lauren reached out. As her fingers closed over the stone she felt a tingling sensation in her scalp and looked up to see the Albino stallion at the head of the fall. He was watching her.

In a split second, Lauren was on her feet. She reached for her stirrup and finding the pebble still in her hand, dropped it into her jacket pocket. "Come on, Lightning!" she urged, as she swung into the saddle. "We mustn't lose him this time!"

The Albino led them higher up the mountain, through regions Lauren had never been before. Each time they reached a clearing, Lauren pushed Lightning into a gallop, but the white

One pebble glittered dully in the water!

horse kept ahead of them. He was always just out of range. After an hour, Lightning began to tire. Lauren glanced at her watch. It was time she should think of turning for home. But which way was that? The forest looked the same in every direction.

Ahead of her, the Albino flicked his tail provocatively and then turned down an open stretch of grass and swung into a canter.

Her last chance! Lauren put Lightning into a gallop, wedged herself into the saddled and lifted the rope. Closer, closer . . . she could see the strands of silver shining in the stallion's mane. Her arm went back. As the rope flew forward, the Albino ducked off the track. Lightning skidded to a halt and plunged after him, only to be stopped short by a barrier of fir trees.

Lauren drew breath, pulling in the rope. She was sure he had turned down here, but there wasn't a sign of him, not even a few hairs where he had pushed through the trees.

Lauren raised the rope ready to throw

She sat in silence, listening for his movements but could hear only the familiar bleating of distant sheep. Lightning pricked his ears and turned back, making his own way down to the valley.

In no time at all they were back at the house. Lauren jumped to the ground and tied Lightning to the corral fence. She found her parents at table, already eating supper.

"Pa, come out and saddle up," she pleaded. "There's an Albino stallion just above the house. I've been trying to catch him all day."

"Not that tale again! I've told you, Lauren," said Myra Berger, her eye on the trail of needles dropping out of Lauren's jacket, "there are no horses left in the forest. It must have been a stray sheep."

"It was a horse – I'm not blind!" persisted Lauren.

"Calm down!" her mother told her.

"You look like you've been climbing trees all day," remarked Kelly from

beneath the new perm she'd had done especially for her Rodeo Queen ride.

"Get those clothes off right now," ordered Lauren's mother and Lauren shrugged out of her jacket and kicked off her boots. She stamped upstairs to shower and change into clean jeans and a sweatshirt. No-one would ever help her catch the horse because no-one believed he existed. She'd never manage on her own. It was impossible!

Lauren would have quite forgotten about the pebble in her pocket had her parents not presented it to her at breakfast next morning. "Can you remember where you found this stone, Lauren?" her father asked. "In Bright Creek, where the Albino lives," she answered sourly.

"Sure?" She looked up, catching the excitement in her father's voice and wanted to know about his special interest. "I took it to Mr. Cairn first thing this morning, on a hunch," he explained and added: "Lauren, it's pure silver!"

It was mid-day when Lauren and her father reached Bright Creek. Lauren kept her eyes peeled for the horse, but saw no sign of him either going out or coming back home. Her father was preoccupied with the nugget. It would surely help to save the farm.

"Dave! Lauren!" Myra Berger ran across the grass, waving to the two riders on returning home. "The old mare, Tammy ... she's foaling. I've rung for Mr. Rice but he's at the rodeo. It could be hours before he gets here!"

Lauren reached the foaling box first. She looked over the door and felt her breath catch in her throat. Lying beside the bay mare was a pure white colt. "Well I never!" Lauren's father whispered as he joined her at the door.

"An Albino!" murmured Lauren dreamily. An Albino line – this colt could found it.

"What shall we call him, Lauren?" her father asked.

"Silver!" she said. "What else!"

Lauren remained at Tammy's door

long after her parents had returned to the house. There would be no need to look for the Albino horse again. A memory of her father's stories had given her the answer and told her why she would never catch him, why he never left any prints. The Indians had bred a herd of white horses. Only the ghosts of Bright Creek could explain the mystery of the silver stallion that had appeared to Lauren and given the family the means to ensure white horses would roam again in that special valley.

Two for One

"Surely it is my turn by now, Ben!" Cheryl Walker argued as her brother turned right for Bydale.

"Not until five past nine - it's only three minutes past," Ben told her and pulled back his jacket sleeve to show his sister the watch.

"I bet you wind it back," she hissed.

"If you wore yours you'd be able to time me," he grinned.

Cheryl grunted, but said nothing. Her watch had not been worth carrying since it fell in the molasses last week. She hated having to walk to shows. Sometimes her mother would give her a lift to the showground, but that only meant wandering around at the other end feeling useless with nothing to do but wait for Ben and Harlequin.

A lorry rumbled up the hill they had just climbed and sounded its horn. Ben touched Harlequin's ribs and praised him when he moved onto the verge. Cheryl turned and lifted her hand, forcing a smile to her lips when she recognized her classmate in the cab.

"It's not fair," Cheryl complained, watching the horsebox shrink into the distance. "How come Elizabeth Robson gets ferried around with two ponies when we have only half of one each."

"We could still beat her," claimed Ben. "Harlequin is steadier these days."

"Pigs could fly!" muttered Cheryl. "Harlequin is not and never will be a nippy gymkhana pony or a serene show hack." Cheryl sighed. She should not complain. If it hadn't been for

Cheryl wished she had Harlequin to herself

Uncle Lennie's new mare being unexpectedly discovered in foal, she and Ben wouldn't have a pony at all. Uncle Lennie presented them with the leggy skewbald as a joint Christmas present when Harlequin had just turned two years old. That was three years ago now. Cheryl and her brother had trained and broken the pony themselves under the eagle eye of their Riding Club instructress.

Cheryl loved Harlequin very much, but that did not make her blind to the fact that he was useless for competitions. You couldn't win show classes with a skewbald, steer your speedy way around the handy pony course on a green five year old, or tackle gymkhana games from a small hunter. Cheryl pulled the rein and brought Harlequin to a stop. "It really must be my turn now!" she pleaded.

Cheryl was entered in the riding pony class. The hack had taken the tickle out of Harlequin's toes and she had high hopes for him until she went

into the ring. It was then she noticed the perfect turn-out of the other riders and the rows of immaculate plaits where Harlequin's multi-coloured mane hung loose and dancing in the wind.

The ride went into trot. Harlequin tossed his head, telling Cheryl it would be more fun to canter. She sat deeper into the saddle, feeling on each rein until he steadied, but the trot was unbalanced and she knew he was resisting her every step of the way.

The judge called the first pony in. Cheryl saw the perfect curve of Jewel's neck, the square halt and the smirk on Elizabeth Robson's face. An upset feeling caught at Cheryl's stomach and crept into her throat. Her eyes burned. Her lips sucked in. It was stupid to go on. She was making herself a laughing stock.

Abruptly, Cheryl turned out of line and cantered Harlequin through the gap in the fence, blinking hard as the field blurred through her tears.

"Cheryl!" Ben ran after his sister. "What's the matter?"

"I'm sick of it!" she cried. "I'm sick of being at the end of every line and having Elizabeth make snide remarks all the following week. We never ever win, Ben!"

"We will, we will," he said. But they did not. Harlequin was a good all rounder and keen, but there was always a better horse in the class. The only rosettes they ever won were for clear round jumping, in which Harle-

quin had no one to compete with but himself.

On Thursday, Ben cycled into town to pick up some shopping for his mother and buy the evening paper. He did not usually pay much attention to the pony magazines, as they seemed to be written for girls. But, on this occasion, the front cover caught his eye – two riders, one horse it said. Ben picked the magazine out and took it to the counter.

Ride-and-Tie sounded the perfect

competition for them. Cheryl, however, did not agree.

"Run three miles! Three! Forget it, Ben," she almost laughed.

"Cheryl, it's made for us," her brother insisted. "Harlequin is just the right sort of horse, big but steady and he knows both his riders."

"I don't want a rosette so badly I'm prepared to run three miles myself to chance my luck!" Cheryl stated and marched out. Ben sent off for the competition list anyway. When he discovered there was to be a regional trial at Stakesby, only fifteen miles away, he purposely left the list where Cheryl would find it. The trial featured special prizes for young competitors and family teams. Ben hoped that would change his sister's mind. It helped, but the deciding factor was the discovery that Elizabeth Robson was going. Whatever Harlequin's faults, Cheryl was sure the pair of them could manage Ride-and-Tie better than Elizabeth and Jewel.

When she saw the list Cheryl changed her mind!

September seemed a long way off when they started training, but all too close when they saw the time it took them to run a mile. For the first week, running reduced them to groaning cripples. "We're mad," Cheryl moaned as she flopped against the gate. "Completely mad!"

After a week, the training became a little easier. Their legs still ached at the end of the day but their times were visibly improving. By the middle of August, Cheryl found she no longer hated every step. Ben was actually enjoying it.

September came and with it confirmation of their entry. The schedule and course map arrived on Friday morning. Cheryl followed the dotted route across fields, through forestry and over the banks and streams. "But how are we going to get there?" she asked, her enthusiasm vanishing. "Stakesby is fifteen miles away."

"I've booked a trailer for the day," said their father, Mr. Walker. "It's a

big competition and I want to see you two win. You could do without the handicap of walking there if you are going to get round the course."

Mr. Walker drove slowly to Stakesby; he was not used to handling the car with such a heavy load behind. All the same, they arrived in good time. "No question of walking the course first," Cheryl joked as she stooped to remove the wadding from Harlequin's brushing boots and restrap them for the ride. Ben exercised the skewbald. He walked him in circles to loosen up his joints, talking to him quietly until he settled and stopped neighing at all the excitement.

Cheryl mounted five minutes before the whistle called the novice class to the starting line. As the competitors began to gather, she pulled off her track suit top, told her arms they would be warm once the race started and fastened the chin strap of her crash cap.

The starter lifted his pistol. Out of the corner of her eye, Cheryl saw Elizabeth Robson was mounted on her father's point-to-point horse. She tightened her heels, tickling Harlequin's sides. "Come on boy, we must beat Elizabeth today!"

"Three ... two ... one!" The thoroughbred went up on its hindlegs. The pistol fired and Harlequin leapt out of the lines. Cheryl pushed Harlequin up to the front. Her own running would need every advantage she could find. Some of the horses were

Harlequin leapt out of the lines

trotting. Elizabeth was finding her thoroughbred a handful and kept going off course. Cheryl reached the first stop and leapt to the ground. Harlequin stood patiently, well practised at the routine, while his first rider raced away and he awaited Ben.

Onto the horse and off again. They were making very good time running and riding in turn. Finally Cheryl was running down to the end of the woods. She counted her strides to keep pace. The fields opened. Over the fence. Someone was coming behind her. Cheryl forced her legs to go faster. She must stay in front. Her lungs stabbed with each breath and her thighs were leaden. A flash of brown and white brought Ben home on Harlequin. Cheryl flung herself forward and suddenly her legs were running for themselves. The crowd engulfed her, applause broke like waves – it was over.

Cheryl and Ben sat in tandem on Harlequin's back for a photograph.

Red and gold ribbons fluttered on Harlequin's browband.

Mrs. Walker edged to the right and lifted the camera again. "I'm sure Harlequin's smiling," she said.

"I wouldn't be surprised!" laughed Cheryl. Ben patted Harlequin's ribs. "I always said he was a winner."

"It was just a question of finding the right competition!" agreed his sister.

A Bit
Special

"Mintaka jumped a four-foot wall with me this week. Mrs. Anderson said she thinks we'll be good enough to join the riding school team next year – I hope so. At the end of the lesson she got me to put Mintaka over the jumps again, to show the eleven o'clock novices who had just arrived how to place a horse correctly. Must say, Mintaka is a bit of a handful when there is an audience in sight. I made him trot circles until he settled down, then went over the course again. He jumped like a stag!"

Lisa put the pen down, feeling her cheeks burn as she scanned the letter. She then looked up at the small bay thoroughbred miniature that pranced along her bedroom windowsill.

This was Mintaka!

The jumping lesson she was describing to Sally was real enough, except that it was one of Mrs. Anderson's working pupils who had given the demonstration while she hung over the wall with the other hopefuls.

She had never intended to lie to Sally, it had just happened that way. Learning to canter and the success of being able to tighten her girths from the saddle, seemed so tame and boring after reading Sally's first letter. It was all about the gymkhana she had been to and how her Clarentina had almost won a showing class, but had been unnerved by a balloon bursting at a crucial moment.

If Sally ever knew how ordinary her rides were, Lisa was quite sure that she would not bother to write back. So, she let her imagination add to the truth a little. She didn't *have* to pretend that she actually had a pony. Living in the city, Sally would have understood she may not manage that, but Sally wasn't going to think of her as a horse-dunce, not if Lisa could help it!

Perhaps if Clarentina had been a more ordinary pony it would have been easier, but she sounded terrific. The drawings Sally sent of her pony proved it. Clarentina was not the thatch-maned Dartmoor Lisa had expected to encounter when she replied to the pen-pal advertisement from Ashburton. She was a beautiful riding pony with fragile legs and a delicate face.

Out in the garden, Sam began to bark. When Lisa let him in, she lingered a moment, looking at the long lawn and the fruit bushes beyond. Five years ago she had thought that garden big enough to keep a pony in. Now, she knew that she would never have a 'back garden' pony. The most she could

on the doormat. "Dear Lisa," she wrote, "I was so sad to hear about your arm. I am afraid I will have to disappoint you over Clarentina. You remember I said about breeding a foal off her? Unfortunately she'll be away at stud next week so you will miss her. But never mind, I'm borrowing two Darties from Mr. Roberts down the hill. They are very well behaved, so you will be able to come trekking. I am sure you will be able to ride if we stick to a walk. See you Monday. Love, Sally."

Clarentina would not be there! Lisa stared at the letter in disbelief and then sat down heavily and groaned. If only she had not bothered writing, just waited to tell Sally when they met. Now, her 'bad wrist' meant they would have to spend the week at walking pace instead of galloping together over the moors!

Sally and her father met Lisa at Exeter station. Sally was rather stouter than Lisa had imagined, and looked very 'farmy' in jeans and a home-knit

sweater. Her ruddy-complexioned father was every bit a man-o'-the-land. She managed to catch the words 'Sally' and 'Lisa' in his speech, but he had such a thick accent that she had to make do with nods and smiles and hope for the best.

"How's your arm?" Sally asked as they sped out of town. "Much better, thanks," Lisa was able to report. "The doctor said that if I take it steady, I'll be fully recovered by the end of the week." Let's be sure of a few canters at least, Lisa thought.

They reached the farm just as the sun was dipping to glow on creeper-covered walls and the sloping fields beyond. Mr. Coombes drove round into the yard and parked the car in a shed beside two tall tractors. Mrs. Coombes met them at the kitchen door. She smiled broadly. "Did you have a good journey down, Lisa?" she asked.

"Yes, thank you," Lisa replied politely, trying not to stare too obviously as she searched for any signs of horses. "The train was right on time," said Sally.

Hearing her voice, a pony neighed across the yard. Automatically, Lisa turned to look. Mrs. Coombes laughed. "I was going to get the supper ready, but I daresay you'd rather visit Clare first," she said.

"Clare . . .?" Lisa breathed in, her forehead puckering. She looked at Sally who immediately ducked past, muttering something about changing her shoes. "Get some boots for Lisa too," her mother called after her.

Sally was silent when she returned and refused to look Lisa in the eye. Was

Mrs. Coombes met them at the door

Clarentina still here, Lisa wondered. If so, why was Sally trying to keep her secret. She couldn't understand it. Lisa followed Sally across the yard, through the hayshed and into a low-roofed building. There, wooden partitions separated two Dartmoor ponies. "The black one is Clarentina," Sally confessed with a shrug.

Open-mouthed, Lisa stared at the twelve-hand mare. She was pretty-faced with a neat build and soft dark eyes, but Lisa's mind could not match her to the aristocratic fourteen-two pony in the pictures she'd received.

"She is every bit as good as I told you," said Sally, still refusing to look up. "When you started telling me about Mintaka, I thought I'd better make her sound a bit more special. All my friends say I should move onto a bigger horse now, but I couldn't bear to part with her. I thought you would say the same if you knew."

A guilty flush crept over Lisa's neck. Sally pointed to the bay. "This is

Bobby. He's a bit ancient, but tough as old boots. At least with two I thought we'd be able to ride together. That's if he's not too small for you. I know you aren't used to little ponies, but with your wrist ..." Sally's voice wavered on the verge of tears.

"Actually, he's just my size," Lisa admitted. "It's Mintaka who is on the small side."

"You mean you don't ride a proper thoroughbred?" Sally turned, her eyes misty with tears of shame.

"I ride whatever the eleven o'clocks are given and it is never over thirteen hands," confessed Lisa. "Mintaka is too small even to make that because he's five inches high and lives on my windowsill."

Sally's tears turned to laughter. "I'm so glad," she said. "I thought you'd be picking faults with Clare all week. I was furious when Mum wrote to you!"

The worries of both girls vanished and Lisa began to smile. They had led each other quite a dance with their tales, but it would be all right now. Lisa reached out to stroke Bobby's grey-stippled nose, feeling wonderfully happy. There'd be no clear rounds with him, but the touch of a real live pony was preferable to Mintaka's cold, glazed coat any day.

Never Again

Screaming engines shook the air. Princess leapt to one side, dragging the reins through Karen's hands. The pony's ears were flat against her head. Her neck was stiff, her nose was in the air. Karen Elliot's body stiffened with fear as the little mare became wooden and she felt the madness of panic. "Steady, steady girl, it's all right!" Karen might as well have been talking to herself. Princess was deaf to everything but the whistling wind as she began to bounce, her coat white flecked. Karen knew she did not have the strength to hold the mare back much longer.

The roaring plane skimmed the trees. Everything went black for an instant as Karen's eyes shut and she crouched instinctively. Princess went up on her hindlegs and then she was off and away. Her iron-shod feet rang a frantic beat against the tarmac.

"Princess, stop, stop!" cried Karen as she hauled at the reins. The leather slid through her helpless fingers and Princess only ran faster. The main road suddenly appeared. A big lorry was coming, towering above them as its brakes shrieked. Princess swerved, but was not fast enough . . .

Karen sat up with a start, tears streaming over her cheeks, her body shaking. The bedroom was dark and still. Outside, an owl hooted before flying into the night. She rubbed her eyes. The nightmares had haunted her for the first month after losing Princess, but she had thought they

Princess reared up on her hindlegs

were at an end. She slid out of bed,
wrapping her arms about her to keep
warm. Beyond the lawn and the hedge
of cotoneaster stood the sheds. One
was full of tack, feed and gardening
equipment. The other, with its half-
doors latched, was empty, swept out
and disinfected. Karen's eyes pricked
again. There would never be another
pony to match Princess.

The next morning Karen felt shat-
tered. She had not slept well for the rest
of the night and her blotchy, white face
showed it. Her mother had noticed, but
said nothing. She'd given up asking
about the nightmares weeks ago.
Karen knew that her mother thought
there was something unnatural in
them having lasted so long. She could
not seem to make her mother understand
that Princess had been special, not just
any horse. She had been bought as a
twelfth birthday present and they had
shared so much together.

Retreating to her bedroom, Karen
pulled out her photograph album and

turned the pages lovingly. Princess on the day she arrived! Their first rosette! Going over the jumping course her father had set up for them in the paddock!... you couldn't replace a pony like that – she was in a class of her own.

"Karen!" At the sound of her mother's voice Karen closed the album and went to the door. "Will you come and give me a hand in the garden please?"

Reluctantly, Karen pulled on her

boots and went outside. She knew that her parents were doing what they thought was best, but she wished they wouldn't try so hard. She did not feel ready for another horse yet and sometimes she thought she never would be. Princess had meant so much. It was hard to explain to someone who had not been through it, but her death had come as a complete shock. One day they had been together, with Princess brimful of life and eagerness. The next, she was dead and Karen felt she had been robbed.

She had hardly got outside the house when she heard hoofbeats on the drive. She caught her breath and shut her eyes as she struggled to regain control over her feelings. When she opened them it was to come face to face with a plump bay pony of around thirteen hands. Rough-coated and solid, she recognised him at once as Danny, one of the old faithfuls from Mr. Paget's trekking centre. Karen said nothing. She did not move and the

smile on Mr. Elliot's face began to fade.

"Mr. Paget asked if we would take him over the winter," her mother said, coming to the rescue.

Karen nodded. "I'll put him in the field then," she offered.

Her father's face fell. He had hoped for something more enthusiastic and Karen wished she could find it in herself to look happier. She hated to upset them, but she did not want another pony. It was as simple as that.

Every one that came along was like rubbing salt in the wound. Karen gulped. There was only one thing she wanted – to have Princess back.

Three weeks passed during which Karen went through the motions of looking after Danny. She fed him, mucked him out and checked his feet daily, but she did not ride him. She couldn't think of him as her own. Her mother would watch her, feeling both annoyed and disappointed. Karen guessed it would not be long before she was cornered over this, and she was proved right the following Saturday.

"Bit brighter today," Mrs. Elliot said at breakfast. "Why don't you take Danny out? It would do him good to get a change of scenery."

"I thought he was here for a rest," Karen replied, knowing full well that Mr. Paget preferred the ponies to be worked lightly over the winter to ensure they didn't slip into bad habits.

Her mother turned back to the table. Her brow was creased and her lips

pressed tightly together as she tried to find the right words. "Look, Karen, you can't carry on like this. Wishing isn't going to bring Princess back. There's a good pony out there going to waste so why don't you shake yourself out of this and enjoy him."

"Because I don't want him!" Karen snapped. "I never asked for him, so leave me alone!"

"But, Karen, you did so well with Princess . . ."

"Just leave it will you!" Karen's

temper finally went over the edge. "I don't want another pony. There'll never be a replacement for Princess. Never!" She ran from the room, tears streaming down her cheeks. Princess ... her one true friend ... how she missed her.

Karen grabbed her coat, pulled on her boots and ran out of the house. She must have walked for miles, right out of Thurston and on until she came to Tany Wood. There she felt better and it was almost as if Princess was with her. The dream vanished a moment later when she turned a corner to come face to face with a small skewbald pony tethered to the grass verge.

Karen's eye judged him to be about thirteen-two though he looked smaller. His ribs were stark under a scruffy coat that sprouted winter tufts and clots of mud. Bare patches on either side of his tail and a rubbed-away mane were a testament to lice. His feet were long and chipped. Pink sores showed where his halter had rubbed. The skewbald

Never Again

The skewbald was tethered to the grass verge

lifted his head and regarded Karen with sad resignation, then resumed chewing a nettle root.

Her heart seemed to explode with anger and sadness. It was such a pathetic sight. Without realising she had moved, Karen found herself across the lane and at the pony's side, emptying her pockets and rubbing the stubby neck. The pony looked at the offering of sugar cubes as if he couldn't believe this was really happening. Then he grabbed for them and nudged Karen hopefully for more.

"I'm sorry, poppet, that's all I've got left." Karen's fingers strayed along the wet coat. He was shivering. Giving up the quest for titbits, the pony began to nuzzle Karen's coat and lick her hands. She smiled and patted him. "Just wait here and I'll bring you something to eat," she told him as she turned for home.

"Karen! Where have you been? I thought you were upstairs," said Mother seeing the wet clothes and muddy boots. "Sit yourself in front of the fire and we'll get you dried off."

Karen shook her head and said, "What can you do about cruelty to ponies?"

Her mother stopped in her tracks. "What do you mean?" she asked.

Out it all tumbled – the state of his coat, the sores, long feet, no food. "It really is that bad?" her mother wanted to know.

"Oh, Mum, it's awful," cried Karen. "Really, I'm not just being soft. Only I

don't know who the pony belongs to so I couldn't do anything."

Her mother nodded. "I'll call the R.S.P.C.A. and they will see to it," she said. "You'll have to explain exactly where you saw the pony."

"What if they can't do anything unless it's actually being beaten . . . can't we take it away? There's room in our field for two ponies," cried Karen with visions of the owners promising to buy food and bed up a stable, then wriggling out of it all by saying they hadn't meant to do any harm.

Her mother was adamant. "It's better that they handle this," she insisted. "They know how they stand with the law. It will only cause problems if you get involved, Karen."

Karen shrugged and left the room. Her mother assumed she had gone up to change, but Karen had other plans. There was quite a bit of money in her piggy-bank upstairs, enough for a deposit and a show of goodwill at least. She folded the notes carefully, pushed

them deep into her jeans pocket and set off for Tany Wood. It took longer to get there than she had expected and when she reached the verge the skewbald pony had gone. For a moment she panicked but then remembered there would be a trail of prints.

Karen searched the ground, found the crescent shaped depressions in the mud and jogged down the lane in pursuit. The skewbald was being led by a plump middle-aged woman in a heavy coat and wellingtons. "Wait!"

Karen called, and she began to run. The woman turned, looking worried. The pony recognised Karen's voice and whickered softly, bringing a smile to her lips.

"Is this your pony?" asked Karen. The woman nodded and looked at the girl suspiciously, her small eyes inching across Karen's face.

"Would you sell it?" was Karen's next question.

"Sell?" repeated the woman.

"Yes!" Karen nodded enthusiastically. Her heart was pounding. Already it was as if the pony was hers. She couldn't explain why, but she felt she had to have it.

The woman looked at the pony then back at Karen. She gave a little smile. "Do your parents know about this idea, pet?" she asked. Karen lied baldly, desperation giving her the courage to smile as she ploughed ahead. "They said it was all right and I've got the money now," she said.

The woman's lip pulled in as she

"I've got the money now," Karen said

sighed: "Where do you live, honey?"
"Mayfield, in Witton, on the end of the
High Street," Karen told her.

The woman patted the pony. "I'll be
sad to part with him, but I'm not blind
to the fact we can't afford to keep him
any longer. I'll come over to see your
parents, just to make sure," she said.

"It will be all right, I promise,"
exclaimed Karen, "and he'll have a
good home."

The woman nodded. "My daughter
Jenny will be up in arms about this,"
she told Karen, "but it's her own fault.
She never would listen when I told her
how much work was involved in
keeping animals. As for the cost, who'd
have thought something so small
would eat so much. Jenny's too lazy,
that's her trouble!"

Karen's fingers were itching to take
the rein and then at last the woman
handed him over. "You might as well
take him now. It will be easier than
coming down just to go back again,"
shrugged the pony's owner.

There were arguments when Karen got back. Her mother was at first flabbergasted, then angry that she had gone behind her back, and then aloof. It didn't take her long to come round though, not once she saw the interest her daughter was taking in the new arrival. The little pony helped because he had a way of winning affection and after a very short time Mrs. Elliot was following the habit of the rest of the family in taking him out little treats.

Karen had her work cut out, but she

loved every minute of it. Dealing with Troubador was something new and special. She pulled on rubber gloves, cut the pony's mane to a stubby ridge and liberally covered him in de-lousing powder. A dose of worming powders put weight on him and with good food given daily and a warm stable in which to sleep, he soon put on condition.

Karen smiled. It did not feel wrong to have Troubador in Princess's stable. Unlike Danny, who would be happy enough with anyone, Troubador really needed her.

Off to a Bumpy Start

Elaine's heart was thudding and her hands made sticky marks on the bus ticket clutched in her fingers. A girl in jodhpurs got up from the front seat and went to stand by the doors as the bus stopped. Elaine followed her, hanging back and hoping she would not be seen. Last week, Natalie and Janet Smith had made fun of her because she didn't know the difference between a bridoon and a curb rein. She didn't want it to happen again.

There were five minutes to get through before the lesson would start. Elaine's legs trembled. Her throat was dry. Now, she could smell the horses and the sawdust. Her ears filled with the sounds of hoofs scraping concrete and the low whickers of ponies in conversation.

Yesterday, in her imagination, she had been performing flying changes on Florette and accidentally been given Tinder Box the ex-racehorse, to ride. She had mastered him effortlessly. Things were very different now that she was actually at the stables and the horses were real.

Two cars came into the yard and deposited a batch of eager young riders. It was hard for Elaine to understand how they could be so excited when she just felt sick with worry before every ride. Had they forgotten how Scamp bucked Amanda off last week? Or were they all so brave it did not bother them?

Across the yard the office hatch

In her imagination Elaine won races!

opened and Denise Carlton's dark head appeared as the queue formed hastily outside. They all stood there, ears straining, hoping their favourite pony would not be allotted to someone else. The girl behind Elaine echoed her sigh of relief as awkward, fiery Florette was allocated to the jodhpur-wearing girl from the bus. Elaine's spirits lifted. Perhaps she would be lucky and get Bongo again. He wasn't particularly nice, but at eleven-hands she did not have far to fall.

The line moved on. "Who did you get?" asked the girl in front of Elaine. Her friend screwed up her face. "Bongo!" she replied and Elaine's heart sank.

Then it was Elaine's turn. Denise looked her up and down through narrowed eyes, consulted her list, chewed the top of her pencil and came to a decision: "You can try Pearl this week. Anne will help you tack her up!"

The smaller ponies were all ready for the lesson. Anne, a working pupil, ran

Off to a Bumpy Start

"You can try Pearl this week," Denise said

round getting any additional mounts ready if needed. Elaine discovered her in the tack room, forcing rubber treads onto stirrup irons.

"Hello, who've you got this time?" asked Anne.

"Pearl!" Despite her best intentions, Elaine's voice quavered and she flushed.

Anne smiled. "You needn't be scared of her. Pearl's a real softie." Anne left the stirrups, hooked a saddle and bridle over her arm and dashed across the yard leaving Elaine to trail after her.

Pearl was tethered in the pony stalls. She was about thirteen hands high and pure white with a thick-set tail and full curly mane. She nudged Anne and gazed at Elaine with an expression of bored resignation. "There you are," Elaine told herself, "she couldn't be quieter." All the same, the butterflies in her stomach kept on fluttering.

Anne positioned the saddle, hooked the girth under and had it fastened in a moment. Then, the bridle was on, the

throatlash fastened and the reins were handed over.

Elaine stood alone with the pony. Her hand shook as she patted the mare's neck and whispered: "Hello, Pearl!" She was a much bigger pony than Bongo. Elaine could barely see over her withers. She knew Anne had been trying to reassure her by saying that Pearl was a quiet pony, but that was with other people riding her, people who knew what they were doing. There was no telling what she

91

would be like for this lesson under the control of an idiot such as herself.

Denise strode into the covered school and ordered the ride to mount. She looked as if she had just left the army with her smart jodhpurs, shining leather boots and that long whip she kept at her side. She sounded like it too, always shouting. Elaine so wished that Anne had been giving the lesson.

With a struggle, she hauled herself into the saddle and followed the file that led out on the left rein. Piebald Scottie was in front, behind him Florette, then Beauty, Linnet, Scamp and Pearl. Bongo and the little Shetland pony, Jolly, brought up the rear.

"Hands lower, Jane! Toes in on Florette, heels further back!" Denise corrected their positions, finding faults with everyone. Elaine tried hard to do as she was told. She forced her heels down so hard it seemed as though the ankle bones would break, but by the time she reached the next corner mirror

they had sneaked back up again. Perhaps she was a hopeless case, she thought.

Jane, on Scottie, was asked to trot. Florette tried to follow her stablemate and her rider, Sarah, turned scarlet in her efforts to hold back the spirited mare. "Hands down with Florette!" Denise called. "Relax! That's better – now let her go!" So they were trotting too. One by one the line in front of Elaine and Pearl shortened until it was their turn. Elaine squeezed hopefully, but nothing happened.

"Don't just sit there!" yelled Denise. "Keep trying!"

What did she think she was doing! Elaine flapped her legs, but quiet Pearl was so quiet she continued to walk. Eventually, miraculously, Elaine caught the mare at the right moment and she lumbered off to the back of the ride without sneaking across the middle of the school as Bongo had done the week before. Midway through the lesson they stopped to do exercises in the saddle. Then, when they were back on the track and Denise asked the whole ride to canter, Elaine knew that the worst was yet to come.

One by one, Scottie, Florette, Beauty and Scamp, cantered off. Pearl showed no inclination to leave the ride and persisted with her trot, getting faster and faster until Elaine could not keep up with her. "Shoulders back!" shouted Denise. "Relax and sit down!" Elaine decided this was impossible, but she must have got it right because Pearl

Elaine knew the worst was still to come

was soon cantering around. Elaine had to cling to the saddle to stay on until she broke into trot again.

More trotting, then suddenly it was over. The ponies turned in. The class dismounted onto shaky legs and the next batch of riders swarmed into the yard. Before leaving Elaine paused and took one last look around, Tinder Box poked his head through the grill and watched her, nostrils flaring. Whatever his reputation amongst the pupils, he was a magnificent horse. Elaine's mind began to drift as she wondered what it must be like to ride him. He was the opposite of Pearl, who wanted to walk all day.

The girl from the bus came up to her in the yard. "Thank goodness we don't have to ride him!" she said with a nod at Tinder Box. "How did you find Pearl?" "I'm afraid I didn't manage very well," Elaine admitted.

Sally shrugged. "I thought you did all right. Florette was awful!" She laughed. "It's not fair is it? As soon as you think you are improving and it is getting to be fun, they go and put you on a harder horse."

Elaine wondered - was it as simple as that? Was it a stepping up to move from Bongo to Pearl? Maybe she had not done so badly after all! Granted, she had not equalled her dreams, but there was always next week to learn to canter properly.

A Taste for Excitement

Pamela, who by now had become Mrs. Benson's star pupil, turned Snowdrop into the centre and trotted straight towards the jump. She dropped the reins and stretched out her arms as the pony skipped the poles and popped over the jump with all the grace of a ballet dancer. Third in line, Julie gulped and swallowed hard. Not that the jump was anything to be scared of, standing eighteen inches above the sawdust and just enough to make sure the ponies got beyond a trot. It was nore Mrs. Benson. She was a stickler for doing things properly and always managed to notice when Julie was gripping the saddle with her knees, or had caught hold of the pommel.

Sweat beaded Julie's brow, making her face cold. Though small, the jump was professional-looking, with painted poles and stands with proper jumping cups. It was most unlike the rustic fence stakes Gillian had put down that time at Oaklands when Topper decided to take the whole lot in one enormous leap. She had finished up with such a bruise that she had needed to take a cushion into school with her the next week in order to sit on the plastic chairs. It had been very embarrassing!

All the same, she missed Oaklands. Mrs. Benson's stables were further away and the rides cost more, but her parents had decided, after the jumping fiasco, that she ought to have a qualified teacher and Mrs. Benson had a string of letters after her name. The prospect was exciting until Pamela actually arrived. Shouldn't grumble, of course, she knew that but, ... well, Mrs. Benson was a bit of a dressage freak and they spent the first three months just walking round and trotting without stirrups. Julie sighed. Oaklands might be more risky but it had been fun and she was sure that she would have been jumping three-foot-six by now and going out for gallops along the beach.

Now she wasn't at Oaklands. She was here and Mrs. Benson was bellowing for her to hurry up, and waving her crop in the air. With a silent prayer, Julie turned Malone towards the poles.

"Drop the reins!" Mrs. Benson's command rang across the school.

Julie's fingers reacted as if the reins had just given her an electric shock. Malone's head went down and he took up that weird springy trot towards the jump, lurched and was over. Malone made a bee-line for the back of the file and Julie had to grab his mane to

"Drop the reins!" came the loud command

stay on. Fortunately, Mrs. Benson was too busy telling the next girl to get her heels down to notice.

After the ride, Pamela met Julie in the yard. "Are you still looking for a pony?" she asked as they walked to the bus stop. Julie's heart leapt. Oh, to have a pony of her own! To get away from riding round the ring all the time! "What have you found?" she asked. Her eyes were bright and her spirits soared despite the fact that Pamela had probably discovered something far too expensive.

"Well, you know Mr. Stakesby who has the farm behind us? He's put Jasper up for sale," said Pamela. "Seems Eileen's suddenly discovered disco-dancing and can't be bothered with him any more. He came round last night to see Mum and ask if I wanted him, but Jasper is far too small and besides he's not really my type of pony. Still, I mentioned you might be interested and said I'd ask. I hope you don't mind."

"Mind!" Julie laughed out loud. "It's fantastic. I'll ask Mum and Dad as soon as I get in."

Jasper would be just right for me, Julie thought, turning in her seat when Pamela got off and craning her neck to see over the houses. The Stakesby's farm was just up beyond the wood. She stretched, squinting at the field nearby and the black smudge that might well be Jasper. She'd been to see him a couple of times with Pamela when they walked her mother's spaniels after tea.

As soon as he heard Pamela's voice he would come bounding up the field, tail up, ears pricked to finish with a great skid and snort. Gleaming dark eyes, a big bushy mane and completely black from head to hoof. Plenty of Dales blood there, Julie reckoned, for he was also pretty shaggy.

She sank back into the seat and rested her head against the shuddering window. In her mind's eye she could see them together, sure-footed Jasper galloping over the moor making the peat boom beneath his big capable hoofs ... hunter trials, he'd be good at that ... and gymkhanas ...

By the time she'd reached Artemisia Close, Julie had a string of rosettes behind her and was stepping up to receive a silver cup from the Mayor.

Mrs. Cooper was busy pressing wings onto butterfly cakes to sell at the Church Bring-and-Buy. She glanced at her daughter when the door opened. "Leave your boots outside until they have been washed, Julie," she ordered.

Dutifully, Julie dumped the boots by the step before washing her hands and sidling over to the table. "Pamela was telling me that black pony behind her house is for sale," Julie began, struggling not to sound too excited.

Her mother wiped buttercream off her fingertips, but said nothing.

"It would be just right for me ... sensible, no trouble," continued Julie. "Pamela would have bought him herself only he's a bit too small for her."

"She is rather tall for her age," Julie's mother agreed and began to pack the cakes into a paper-lined tin.

"She seemed to think it would be quite cheap as long as it was to a good home," was Julie's next comment.

Her mother stopped packing. "But who is going to look after it, Julie?" she asked. "A pony is a big responsibility."

"I'd look after it, I promise," urged Julie. "I've learned all sorts of things from Mrs. Benson."

Mrs. Cooper shook her head slowly and Julie felt the excitement drain away from her. "I don't know, I'd rather you stayed at the riding school where Mrs. Benson can keep an eye on you," she said.

By the end of the afternoon, with the house to herself, Julie had succeeded in overcoming her disappointment and had hatched a plan. Her mother obviously thought she was too immature, so she would just have to prove otherwise. After cleaning the baking tins which her mother had been in too much of a

"A pony is a big responsibility!" said her mother

hurry to do, Julie decided to make a cheese and onion flan for tea. She had a bit of trouble with the pastry at one point and unhappily her flan came out of the oven like a crusty balloon. However, once she had squashed it down and filled it with egg and cheese it looked all right again.

By the time her family returned the flan was crisp and golden looking and the house was filled with the wonderful smell of baking.

"Have you had any more thoughts yet about the pony?" Julie asked innocently as she put her knife and fork together.

Dad looked up from his plate and asked "What's this?"

"Oh, Julie's friend heard of a pony for sale and I told her I'd rather she stayed at Mrs. Benson's a bit longer," explained Julie's mother.

"She's been there a year now and can't stay forever," smiled her father, giving a sly wink. "I think we ought to have a look at this pony. It's about time

our Julie took on something like that."
Her mother sighed. "All right," she
told Julie. "Give Pamela a ring and
find out if this farmer of yours is on the
telephone and when we can go and see
the pony."

Mr. Stakesby was delighted to get
the call and promised Julie a practice
ride to see how she felt about Jasper.
The only hitch was he would be out on
Sunday and they would have to go on
Monday evening. Julie had a whole
day to wait!

It was maddening to think there was
a pony so close and yet she could not do

anything about riding it. When the family went on their Sunday walk that afternoon with Ragamuffin, their undersized labrador from the R.S.P.C.A., Julie found she couldn't even be bothered to throw sticks. All she could think about was Jasper. By next weekend she could be riding along this very track, jumping fallen trees. She imagined Muffin loping at her side as they rode through avenues of pine.

They had not gone far up the grass track to Hanging Stone when the air erupted with shrieks and screams. Mrs. Cooper suddenly turned, slipped and gave a weak cry as two horses with girl riders came thundering round the corner. They charged by, horses mad-eyed with red nostrils flaring and iron feet throwing the soft mud high. One of the girls squealed as her horse ducked under some low branches. Ten seconds later they were gone.

In the silent aftermath, Julie's father called for Ragamuffin who had vanished from sight and was likely to

A Taste for Excitement

*Two girls on horseback came thundering
round the corner*

take a good ten minutes to pluck up the courage to return. Mrs. Cooper sat on the grass, rubbing her ankle and grumbling to herself.

Eventually, Ragamuffin was coaxed back. Mr. Cooper gave his wife a hand to her feet, then offered his arm and they went off back to the car. Julie watched her mother wince each time she put her weight on the sore ankle. Muffin clung close, his head low, his dark eyes suspicious and scared.

Back home, Julie was dispatched to the back step with a bowl of warm water to wash Muffin's feet. Her throat was tight as she rubbed the paws dry. Not a word had been spoken all the way home, but now her parents were on their own in the lounge and that wasn't a good sign. As soon as the job was done, Julie let Muffin into the kitchen. Her father called her through to join them in the lounge. Her mother was sitting on the couch with her feet up. Dad stood in front of the fire fidgeting with the ornaments on the

mantlepiece as he always did when faced with a difficult situation. "Julie, it's about this pony ..." he faltered, glancing at his wife.

The tightness in Julie's throat spread across her chest so she could hardly breathe.

"I know you want one, Julie," her mother said patiently, "but, well, you know I've never been happy with the thought of you riding on your own, without anyone to supervise and after today ... I just think it is too

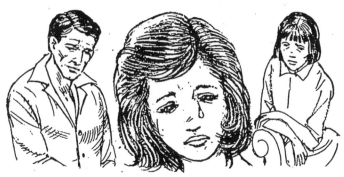

dangerous. The thought of you galloping about like those girls!"

"But I wouldn't ..." Julie's voice quavered. Tears stung her eyes and she had a struggle to keep them back. She shook her head in protest but she could not find the right words.

"We've decided it would be best all round if you stayed at Mrs. Benson's a bit longer," her mother continued. "I couldn't bear to think of you in an accident, Julie." She pulled her mouth into a smile. "It will be better that way, you'll see. You will learn a lot more and it will stand you in good stead for later."

Later, always later! Julie nodded anyway, because there was no point in arguing. If Jasper had never been up for sale it would have been easier, but to have come so close ... Julie ran up the stairs, her teeth cutting into her lip. It was all because of two girls who couldn't be bothered to think of anyone else when they fancied a bit of excitement and a gallop.

Who's Boss?

"Come on, Truant, I've got a super ride planned for today," I cried and as my heels touched the pony's sides he broke into a short-striding bouncy trot. "How would you like to gallop across the moor? I bet you would!" In my mind's eye I could hear the peat pounding underfoot and feel the wind streaming through my hair. We would go up beyond Catnab Rocks and gallop along the sheep tracks as far as Kirkdale where there were ditches to jump.

Although I had owned Truant for almost a month now, I had never been out with him on my own. Melanie, who had a pony in the same field as Truant, was usually out at the same time as me and since she knew all the rides I tended to go around with her.

How I was looking forward to being alone with my pony! No-one to ask for a canter, or to listen to. That was one of the problems with Melanie. Just because she was a year older than me she thought she knew everything about horses. "She's probably jealous," I told Truant as I turned him up the bank. "Anyone can see you are such a handsome pony."

Appearance is not something which should influence you, but it did with me, when I saw Truant. It was love at first sight from the moment he came swanking out of his stable. Welsh Mountain ponies tend to be pretty, but Truant had an impish look about him that was very appealing. Everything about him was special.

On this particular day, we stopped at Catnab Rocks. Down below someone was in the field. I saw one pony leave the group and plod across to the gate. Truant never came to me at a walk. Mind, he didn't come so quickly either. He always seemed to wait until the others were just about to do him out of his pony nuts and then he would streak across, shaking his head at them and bossing them out of the way.

"Come on, Truant, time we got on our way!" I pulled back on the rein. Truant refused to turn. His body seemed to lift under me like a huge spring. "Truant!" My voice was high and the name came out wobbly. My throat closed up. He felt like a different pony ... a wild animal ... completely unpredictable ... I was scared. "Walk on!" I urged, inwardly praying he would become a nice pony again. I touched him lightly with my heels and the next thing I knew I was hanging on for dear life as Truant went up on his hindlegs. "Stop it!" I pleaded. But the instant Truant

He felt like a different pony - a wild animal!

was down he plunged forward and had carried me halfway down the hill before I managed to stop him.

I turned in the saddle. Really, I ought to make him go back. The books always said that, but what about when your pony was rearing. Did it still count? My legs trembled against the saddle. I sensed that Truant was waiting to see if I was going to turn him and I knew exactly what he would do if I touched the rein. "Okay!" I leaned forward and stroked his neck. "It has been a longer ride than usual." I relaxed my hold and touched him to go forward. His muscles relaxed and he trotted happily home.

The following day I kept Truant to the bottom track of the woods that I knew well from my rides with Melanie. Just before we turned back for the field there was a clearing with some very easy to jump gorse bushes.

While he was still in a good mood, I put him into canter and turned off the track. Truant took all of three strides and then stopped, sending me up his neck. It was exactly the same as the last time. I felt him turn wooden underneath me. His head went up and his quarters bunched down. My mouth went dry. I looked at the jumps. Was it

worth it? My legs touched Truant's sides and up he went, snorting angrily. When he touched the ground I shortened the reins to stop him bolting, but he just put his chin against his chest and started plunging around. The moment my hold slackened he reared again.

"Stop it!" I screamed. Tears squeezed out from my eyes and I couldn't stop shaking.

"Don't let him get away with it, Val!" came a familiar voice.

Melanie! Oh no, she would turn up now! I shut my eyes and tried to blink away the tears. Truant heard Melanie's Blaze whinny, and ran over to him. "You must not let him get the better of you," Melanie repeated. "If you do, he'll just get worse."

"I tried to make him jump, but he just keeps rearing," I explained. My heart was thudding for I was sure I knew what Melanie was going to say next and I knew what would happen – Truant would rear really badly, throw me off and then gallop back to the field.

"You have to get him over it now you've started," insisted Melanie. "You can't let him beat you!"

"You can say that, sitting on Blaze, he never misbehaves!" I said scornfully.

"I'll try Truant if you want,"

I was terrified Truant would throw me!

suggested Melanie.

"You do that!" I snapped. This will show her, I thought smugly, as I took Blaze's rein.

Melanie mounted and set Truant at the jump. He wouldn't go. He wouldn't take one step away from Blaze.

"Move Blaze over and out of the way," ordered Melanie.

As soon as I did, Melanie shortened her reins, keeping her hands high. Her legs seemed to wrap around Truant. The grey pony threw his head in the air and started dancing about. Melanie kept him facing the jump. When she kicked him on he reared. The crop made an arc through the air and landed with a thwack on Truant's rump. He reared again. Melanie lifted her arm and he immediately jumped two steps forward. Melanie tried to keep him going but he dug in his heels and reared again. Melanie leaned forward, letting the reins go slack until he came down again. Open mouthed, I watched as suddenly it dawned on me that Truant's rears, though they felt scary, hardly took him off the ground. He actually lifted his forelegs higher when he was jumping. Melanie kept trying and abruptly Truant's neck softened and he popped over the jump.

"Phew! What a performance!" gasped Melanie as she rode Truant back,

patting his neck enthusiastically. "He's just testing you out – new ponies always do."

Melanie dismounted and held out the rein. Reluctantly, I remounted my pony and told him: "Okay, Truant, I'm not going to let you scare me this time!"

Truant trotted towards the jump and stopped. Sensing he was going to rear, I was ready for him this time and leaned forward as Melanie had done. Patience, I reminded myself as fear gripped my stomach. I had to keep him facing that jump and eventually he would give in. Truant reared three times before his head came down and he jumped.

"Well done!" shouted Melanie.

"I did it!" I laughed, clapping my hand to Truant's neck.

There would be times in the future when Truant would rear, but it would never be as difficult again. As I got to know him better I realised he was different from Blaze. He was bossy for a start and a real show off.

I would have understood his rearing a lot quicker if I'd watched him with the other horses a bit more. He was always putting them in their place and as long as I gave in he would treat me with the same contempt! I laughed as I watched him trot away down the field to graze. I'd never become a lazy rider with Truant to keep me on my toes!

Save our Stables

"**J**ust stand still and behave yourself!" Gayle Elsworth snapped at the black Dales pony dragging her across the yard. She had one foot in the stirrup, the other hopping frantically between puddles. "Comet!" Gayle snatched at the reins and succeeded in making the pony pause long enough to launch herself at the saddle. By the time she touched down Comet was halfway down the drive. "I thought you were supposed to be sweet-tempered and obedient," Gayle chided. "Some hopes!" she added.

However, Comet did suppress his excitement enough to stand when they reached the road and wait for Gayle to give him the signal to walk on. Once they cleared the busy section of road, Gayle put her pony into a spanking trot, turned down the bridleway to Skelling and when the pony bucked she knew that Comet was feeling in top form.

An hour later the pair pounded into the yard at Hazelbush House. Comet let out a bugle of a neigh that shook Gayle's bones from their sockets. Heads appeared at the loose-box doors to issue a chorus of welcome.

"Hi, I thought it was you!" Martine Beal put down the fork she had been using to muck out Bishop's box and followed Gayle into the byre where she tethered Comet in the first of three stalls. "Norah's got a new pony," Martine announced. "Come and look, she's really sweet."

Tucked in one corner of the isolation box was a curry-combed ball of fluff out of which poked four matchstick legs, a Shetland nose and the gleam of two dark eyes.

"Where is she from?" Gayle asked.

"Norah found her wandering along the old railway yesterday," explained Martine. "I spent ages on that coat and she ran to the corner every time the comb tugged."

"So, you've been introduced!" Norah James waved to Gayle from the porch. "Put some hay in the field for them would you, then come up to the house while I put some coffee on."

"Okay!" Gayle took one last look at the Shetland filly then set out for the barn. "How is Delight coming along?" she asked Martine.

"Marvellously! That swelling on her leg has gone right down." Martine's face lit up. "Norah says I can definitely have her at the end of the week!"

"You couldn't have wished for a better Christmas present," laughed Gayle. "No! I've always liked Delight, right from the first day when she came obbling into the yard after that uction. Barbed wire!" Martine smacked her fist against her palm. "If I found who did that to her ..."

"Well, she's better now. Just be glad Norah found her," answered Gayle.

They turned the corner into the barn and stopped suddenly. "Whatever's happened to all the hay?" whispered Martine. "I've never seen her let it get so low. Ten bales – that will barely get them to the end of the week."

"Maybe she's waiting for a delivery," Gayle suggested.

Gayle did not go on. She had a shivery feeling that all was not how it should be. When they went up to the house she could not help but pause in the office leading from the porch. Her eyes caught sight of red capital letters stamped over a hay invoice; FINAL REMINDER. Gayle twitched the corner of the sheet. Beneath it was notice of a bank overdraft and under that a bill from the feed merchant. Gayle knew Mrs. James was always given plenty of leeway, the stables being a charity, but this was serious.

"We've got to do something to stop Hazelbush being closed down," Gayle told Martine and the twins, Pamela and Eileen Murray, when they arrived to help during the afternoon. "Even if they waived these debts it wouldn't save the stables. Mrs. James hasn't got the money to buy in feed for the spring. The horses will starve!"

"And after all she's done!" Martine drew a line in the dust with the toe of her wellington. "What if we all chipped

"We've got to do something," Gayle said

in our Christmas money?"

"It isn't enough," Gayle told them.
"We need to raise enough to buy thirty
bales of hay for a start."

There was a stony silence. It seemed
impossible.

"How about a bazaar?" Eileen
suggested, thinking of the two dozen
marzipan mice she had made for the
Church last Saturday. Gayle shook her
head. "Something more eyecatching,
something everyone would want to be
part of," she said.

"Pony Post," murmured Pamela.

"What?" everyone exclaimed.

"How many people do you know who
leave Christmas postage too late?"
enthused Pamela. "We could do a
special same-day-delivery on Christmas
Eve."

"So how are we going to work it?"
Eileen asked when they gathered
together at Gayle's the following
afternoon.

"One person should ride despatch
and the others collect and deliver in

each town," said Martine. "I worked it out last night. Matchmaker and Trooper would be no good for riding from town to town. They are not strong enough, but Comet would be ideal. Gayle could carry letters from, say, Broughton on to Catton and Skelling. Eileen could ride around the Broughton area, Pamela deliver in Catton and I'd deal with Skelling."

"That's twenty-five miles!" Gayle exclaimed.

"I'll donate a cushion for your

saddle," said Eileen with a chuckle.

Gayle's older sister Faith came in with a tray of tea and biscuits. "Now what are you up to – running away?"

Martine explained their plan.

"You need good publicity to be effective," Faith told them soberly. "I'll call the local newspapers for you tomorrow and see if I can drum up some interest."

Faith talked both the 'Clarion' and the 'Gazette' into announcing their effort and both papers promised to take photographs on the day. Gayle began to panic. She did not like standing up in front of people. She was a behind-the-scenes character, a confirmed shrinking violet. "What if it all flops?" she fretted. "What if it is too much for you Comet, and I make you lame?" she told her beloved pony. Comet caught the worry in her voice and nudged her gently with his soft nose.

The day passed. Their feature went in the paper. Faith presented her sister with an ink pad and rubber

tamp embossed with a galloping
horse at the centre and Hazelbush-
Pony-Post-Appeal in a circle around
he outside. "It will stamp ten
housand letters," she announced
onfidently. Gayle felt her heart sink.

Would they really get that many? She
vent down to the kitchen to work out
he weight and began to think about
ising packhorses.

At school Gayle was called out in
assembly to go on the stage and tell
everyone about the appeal. Her tongue

turned to putty and stuck to the roof of her mouth, but she made herself think of the Shetland filly and forced herself to speak.

At last the holidays arrived and she was able to settle into a routine. Mornings started with sorting and stamping letters. Her spirits began to revive when she found the piles numbered nearer a hundred than a thousand. During the afternoons she would take Comet out for long trotting expeditions to build up his strength then work on converting two plastic shopping bags her mother had donated into waterproof mail-carriers.

On Christmas Eve morning Gayle slept until the alarm clock jangled her from her dreams. She had laid out her clothes the night before to save time and she dressed from her bed to keep contact with the cold morning air down to a minimum. The sky was clear, a blessing since rain would give her double the work, but it would be cold. After breakfast Gayle changed from jeans into jodhpurs, pulling on thick cotton tights beneath and woolly legwarmers over the top.

"I hope your great-grandsire really did carry lead over the Pennines," Gayle told Comet as she loaded letters and small parcels into the saddle bags. "You are going to need every ounce of strength you can muster today."

At nine-thirty Eileen arrived to take the first delivery for Broughton. There was a buzz of anticipatory excitement as the girls mounted up. Comet tried to

buck despite the load and made them laugh. Then they were off and as Eileen turned away, Gayle and her pony were alone on the open road.

Pamela and Matchmaker, who was showing her thoroughbred blood by sweating up before she had even started, were waiting in the square beside the Murray's estate car. Gayle dismounted and stamped her feet to restore the circulation whilst Pamela changed over the bundles of letters and stamped the new mail. A small crowd gathered to watch them remount. Gayle blushed and giggled at their cheer and was swept along by a thrill that made her heart beat like a parade drum.

Out of town Comet settled to a steady trot, only pulling when they turned up to Hazelbush House. Ears pricked, Comet lifted his feet higher, his muscles tightening with excitement. Then the minute he reached the yard, he stopped short. The yard was full of inquisitive people.

Mrs. James had arranged a quiet spot for Comet in the byre so that he could rest properly over lunch. Gayle removed his saddle and ran her hands carefully down his legs, then checked his feet for stones. There would be no rest for her. Mrs. James was making use of the publicity to run a refreshment stall, a raffle and to give a tour of the stables and everyone there wanted to hear from Gayle. By the time the reporters arrived to take down their story, Gayle was sounding just like a croaky record. It was a relief to hear one o'clock strike and be able to slip away to get Comet ready for the return journey.

"Could we have the little pony back a bit," the photographer asked, waving at Martine and Delight.

Martine pulled on the reins asking Delight to back. The mare was nervous and her eyes showed a lot of white. "Oh, no! Don't kick," Martine pleaded as she struggled to contain Delight between hands and heels and still have a smile for the camera.

The shutter clicked. A cheer went up from the crowd. "Tally ho!" cried Gayle and they shot down the road.

Comet soon dropped back to a slower pace as he began to feel the effort of the distance. "Come along, not much further!" Gayle urged. At last, the mail bags were empty and the lights of home twinkled ahead of them. Gayle dismounted and loosened Comet's girth. Her legs trembled from having spent so long in the saddle. "You did a

The photographer was soon busy with his camera

marvellous job," she told Comet late
when she put down his feed and rubbed
him over. "Your friends will b
grateful. Everyone is very proud of you
you know." She ran her hand along th
well muscled neck. "I have to go now
but I'll look in on you later."

They all gathered at Hazelbush tha
evening. Mrs. James had tears in he
eyes when she raised her glass to toas
the girls on their effort. "The Pony Pos
has been a great success," she said
"To commemorate the occasion, I'v
decided to christen our new arriva
Special Delivery."

Everyone laughed at the topica
name for the new Shetland pony
Gayle sipped her drink and found he
smile turning into a yawn. Sh
wondered if Comet would be asleep yet
It had been a long day.

Standards

Amy's hands were trembling with excitement as she stood on one leg in the porch of Thatchfield House doing her best to pull on her riding boots. The others had already reached the yard. Amy stamped her heel to force it through the narrow ankle channel then ran to catch up. They had all been assigned their mounts over lunch, but this was the first time they would see them for real.

Smokey was the name of Amy's mount. She crossed her fingers, hoping he would be smaller than the animals she had seen so far. Although she could ride reasonably well, having been promoted to the eleven-o'clock-ride at High Dyke Stables, Amy always tended to doubt her ability. So, when standing in the yard at Thatchfield and a hundred miles from home, she felt she was the only person who didn't know what to do and her courage fled.

Looking about her, Amy caught sight of twin pairs of denim jodhpurs moving in the direction of the forge. Roger and Penny Carson! Amy slowed, feeling she couldn't ask them for help as they were way above her standard. Besides, they would probably laugh because she couldn't remember where Mrs. Tasker had told her to find Smokey. Roger and Penny were used to more than just a trekking centre for their holidays.

"Last year we went to River Meadows in Dorset," Roger had told them all loftily. "It's a show-jumping establishment, you know. Mrs. Meake

Amy felt her courage ebb

asked Penny to consider joining her team when she leaves school. We were jumping Grade C courses at the end of the week. I can't see that happening here – seems to be all walk, trot and keep your toes in."

"Why did you come then?" Amy had asked innocently.

"Must visit the relatives," Penny winked. "Stick with us if you want some excitement," she told Amy.

Amy nodded, but decided to keep clear of Penny and Roger. She didn't feel good enough for them.

"Looking for Smokey?" Mrs. Tasker's daughter, Fiona, waved to Amy from the tackroom. "You'll find him in the byre, fourth stall down." She pointed to a long iron-roofed building. "He's the smallest we've got, but you should be able to manage. He's really sweet." Fiona smiled. "If you have any problems, come and tell me."

Amy nodded and smiled through her embarrassment. Perhaps Smokey would fit her after all, she thought.

It was dark in the byre after the sunlit yard and it took a while for her eyes to adjust. Smokey was unmistakeable, however, for while most of Mrs. Tasker's animals were around the fifteen hand mark, this iron-grey

gelding stood a neat thirteen two. Amy reached out to pat his rump. "Hello there, Smokey!" The pony turned his head to peer at her. He seemed placid enough, without rolling eyes or bared teeth. The tightness in Amy's stomach eased off one notch.

Placid or not, Smokey remained a full six inches taller than the ponies Amy usually rode and tacking up was not easy when you could barely see over the animal's withers. Not for the first time, Amy wished she was tall for her age instead of a shrimp. Out in the yard she almost asked Fiona for a leg into the saddle, but caught sight of Penny and Roger watching her. If they saw she couldn't even mount on her own, they would never stop laughing at her. Amy gritted her teeth, turned the stirrup and nearly split her jodhpurs performing the necessary gymnastics to reach the saddle.

The first ride took them up onto the moorland. Penny and Roger broke into canter when they were supposed to be trotting and got told off in front of everyone, which didn't please them. "You should never canter on ground you don't know," Mrs. Tasker told the two and then proceeded to explain how important it was to look after a horse's legs.

The first ride took them on to the moorland

"We galloped all the time last year," Amy overheard Penny mutter to her brother. "Sit tight and smile," he advised her. "I have a plan!"

What this plan was Amy did not hear and as far as she could see there was none. Penny and Roger kept to themselves, riding at the back of the line and staying behind to close gates after everyone else had gone through. Soon she forgot about them as there was quite enough to contend with riding Smokey. Four hours was a long time to be out when you were used to riding only an hour's lesson. Before long, Amy was standing on her stirrups to relieve her seat!

The aches eased with time and sitting astride a saddle seemed the most natural way to get around. On Wednesday, Mrs. Tasker took them all to the beach. Penny and Roger stayed with Fiona Tasker and two adult riders who had asked for a chance to gallop, while Mrs. Tasker set off with the rest at canter. Smokey bounded away. Amy

bounced and mentally told herself to relax until suddenly she found herself sitting and following Smokey's rocking beat with perfect timing. She laughed delightedly and even dared to pat Smokey's neck as they galloped along.

All too quickly the days passed by. When Fiona took Friday's ride up onto the forestry land Amy rode in a dream, trying to drink in every last bit of the day. She shut her eyes to strengthen the memory of Smokey's movement and ran her fingers through his soft coat as she whispered to him. Without realising it, her slow progress had taken her back through the line until she wound up riding with Penny and Roger.

"Bored with it yet?" asked Roger.

"What? No! I love riding," exclaimed Amy.

Roger's smile became even more of a smirk than usual. "If you can call Tasker's treks riding," he said. "How often have you galloped this week? Twice! And no jumping, not even a log!"

Amy looked at her fingers clasping the reins. It was true, they hadn't jumped anything.

The ride stopped as Fiona opened the first gate into the plantation. "I'll close it!" Penny shouted out.

"Thank you!" Fiona rode on while Penny dismounted. Amy watched, surprised that the girl had not handled the catch from the saddle. Once the catch was home and Penny remounted their horses began to pull.

"Wait!" hissed Roger, as Amy

started out. "But. . ." spluttered Amy. "Give them plenty of time to get ahead," ordered Roger.

"What do you mean?" asked Amy, perplexed.

"You want to jump, don't you?" chuckled Roger.

Amy flushed, feeling confused. "Yes,

but ..." She looked at the felled trees strewn across a patch where tractors turned. Two of them were awkward and bristling, the third made an inviting jump. But the ground ... Amy bit her lip. They were not supposed to be jumping. "There are deep ruts from the tractors," she pointed out.

"It's nothing," cried Penny.

"Leave her, Penny," called her brother. "Come on, or Fiona will wonder where we've got to." Roger clapped his heels to Snap's ribs and bounded away, flying clean out of the saddle when the horse jumped and landing with a thump. Penny followed. Her Cinnamon hurdled the tree and tripped on landing to come down on his knees. Then they were away, all three of them, galloping up the track and laughing at the exhilaration of speed.

"I should have jumped with them when I had the chance," Amy chided herself as she lay in bed. "I get scared too easily. Mrs. Tasker wouldn't have known."

Cinnamon tripped on landing!

"I have a surprise for you today," Mrs. Tasker announced when they met in the yard for the last ride. "Fiona has volunteered to organise clear-round jumping for those who'd like to try. There's a rosette for everyone who gets round."

"Look after me, won't you Smokey," Amy pleaded with her pony as she led him to the yard. Mrs. Tasker stood by the forge, her hands on her hips. Penny was with her and Cinnamon, Mrs. Tasker pointed at his near fore. Amy stopped to mount and fiddled with her girth as she listened.

"I can't think how he's done it," Penny whined.

"He'll need a month off work with an injury like that, and right in the middle of the season!" groaned Mrs. Tasker, making a closer inspection of Cinnamon's knees.

Amy turned away before anyone remembered that she had ridden with Penny and Roger yesterday. She could not have stopped Penny, she knew that, but all the same her conscience pricked. Amy patted Smokey's neck. At least she had not been stupid enough to hurt him.

"It's your go, Amy," Fiona called out, breaking into her thoughts.

Amy turned Smokey to the jumps, pushed him into trot and aimed him straight at them. Smokey dawdled and jumped the first from trot, picked up speed at the stream and swung into a lively canter. Amy tightened her hold on the reins, her heart jumping each time her pony left the ground.

Later, Amy fingered the cherished rosette and patted Smokey enthusiastically. Out of the corner of her eye she saw Penny leading Cinnamon back to his box and could not help but smile. "Maybe I'm not such a bad rider after all. What do you say, Smokey?" she murmured.

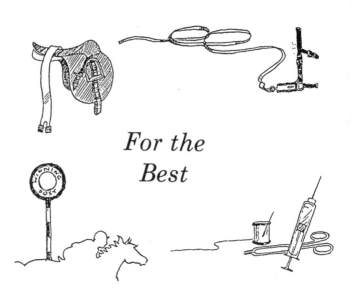

For the Best

Mrs. Dunn looked nervous and her brows pulled together in puzzlement. "She's called Melody," she repeated. Her voice hesitated, not quite sure whether the tears in her daughter's eyes stemmed from happiness or disappointment. "She is big enough, isn't she?" Tracey nodded, choking with the excitement she'd felt the instant she first saw the pony.

Melody was twelve-hands-high, a pretty faced mare with huge dark eyes and neat black feet. Her thick winter coat was flecked through with white hairs that gave her quarters a silvery-blue sheen. A thick wavy tail, matted with burrs, fell to her dark feathered fetlocks. The candyfloss mane made a thatch through which appeared two pointed ears. She was adorable.

"Can I take her for a ride right away?" Tracey asked, shaking with excitement.

Her mother's cheeks flushed and she looked quickly at Tracey's father.

"Well now, Tracey," he replied gruffly, "there's a little snag there, you see ... Melody ... she's ... well, she's not been broken in fully yet."

"Not fully schooled, you mean?" Tracey corrected him, flatly refusing to believe that her parents, sticklers for safety that they were, could possibly have bought an unbroken filly as a first pony.

Mr. Dunn's smile wavered. "Not broken at all, Tracey. She's been handled properly, her manners are lovely and she is old enough to ride,

don't you worry about that. Miss
Thornton would have worked on her
last summer but with the new baby she
didn't have time." He clapped an arm
about his daughter's shoulders. "But
you are not to worry about it one bit. It
will be more exciting this way. Your
Grandad used to say the only way to
get a horse for life was if no one else
interfered first. I remember the first
ride I had on one of his unbroken colts.
What a ride that was. . ."

Tracey switched off from the tale she
had heard a dozen times, her attention
focused entirely upon Melody. Would
the filly be safe in their hands? Ponies
were difficult to break in properly. The
books were always saying how important it was to have them schooled
professionally. Her father had ridden a
lot in his youth when Grandad dealt in
horses, but that was thirty years ago
now. Tracey stroked the pony's velvety
nose. Melody seemed quiet enough and
as her father said, doing it themselves
they could be sure no one handled

Tracey stroked the pony's velvety nose

Melody roughly. They would be with her all along.

". . . he came up from the back and won the race hands down. What a horse he turned out to be. Never had his spirit broken, you see, that's the trick." As her father's voice broke into Tracey's thoughts, she felt a surge of joy burst from her heart. He was as excited about the pony as she was – of course they would manage!

Melody proved a good pupil. She was a lively character, but gentle and co-operative. The ready trust she placed in Tracey and her father made it easy to teach her new lessons. Tracey made a habit of spending an hour with the mare after school and soon had her walking quietly along the bridleways near to home, even lunging in the paddock. Her father's shifts sometimes brought him home for the afternoons and on those days he would take Melody out. Before long, Tracey heard him talking to her mother about getting a saddle for Christmas.

In December, Sedgemere School acquired an extra bus for taking pupils home. Tracey was delighted, as this meant she could get back to Melody fifteen minutes earlier than usual. On the way home that first afternoon she

stared dreamily out of the window, imagining her first ride. Melody would have a lively stride, she would be quick to move up to each new pace and her gallop would be like the wind.

"Hey, Tracey!" Christopher Topping waved and shouted from the front of the bus. "That idiot pony of yours is causing a traffic jam!"

Tracey jumped to her feet and was thrown forward as the coach driver slammed on the brakes. Melody's speckled rump swung into the road. Her hocks were down, her feet spread as she stared wide-eyed at the flapping sheets on Mrs. Johnson's line. The bus driver hooted. Melody backed, her ears flat against the sides of her head. Blood drained from Tracey's face as she saw her father raise his arm to clout Melody for misbehaving. The mare caught him off balance, went up on her hindlegs and whipped the lead-rope out of his hands. Slithering on the tarmac, Melody fled down the High Street. Brakes screamed. "Flamin' nags!" muttered the bus driver. Tracey heard a high-pitched neigh as the frightened pony's legs buckled.

Mr. Smithers, the vet, later betrayed no emotion as he came out of the stable. His blue eyes rested a moment on Tracey's white face and then he

Melody was suddenly among the flapping sheets

addressed her parents. "No broken bones you'll be relieved to hear, but I'm afraid it is touch and go – it might be for the best ..."

Tracey ran from the room. She found Melody lying on a deep bed of straw, her near-hind leg stuck straight out at her side. Strips of flannelette sheet they had used to stem the bleeding while waiting for the vet were coiled upon the straw in one corner. The pain-killing injection had taken the agony from her eyes and she had stopped shaking. Melody whickered softly as Tracey sat down beside her and stroked the soft furry hair that curled upon her forehead. A flood of tears tipped over Tracey's lashes and streamed down her cheeks.

Why had her father been so stupid? Some surprise his plan to traffic-proof Melody had been! Tracey's fingers traced the heavy line of Melody's jaw. The mare grunted contentedly and laid her head in the girl's lap. Her father thought he knew everything there was to know about horses when really he knew nothing! Gulping, Tracey shut her eyes tight. Melody was having to pay the price of his inflated pride with her life. Tracey would never forgive him for this - never!

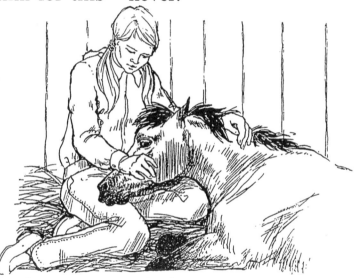

The mare pricked her ears as her drugged eyes struggled to make out the newcomer to the stable.

"Hello, Mum!" Tracey's voice was flat. She felt worn out.

Mrs. Dunn stepped inside and crouched quietly beside her daughter.

"The vet says Melody could recover but she may never really get over this. Her hind legs took such a wallop when she fell ... the joints, well, they might never be the same again. There'll be no hunting or jumping for her, not for a long time anyway. If you want to put her out of her misery, we'll buy you another pony to make up for it." She paused. "Your father's very upset about what happened."

"So he should be! It was his fault!" Tracey's fingers dug into Melody's deep coat. "He's almost killed her!"

Mrs. Dunn drew a sharp breath. "Tracey, please!" She paused. "Look, your father has promised to pay for whatever treatment is needed, but you have to decide and you should know the truth which is that she won't mend easily and it will take a long time and a lot of care."

"I want to keep her," Tracey said stoutly.

"Then I'll tell Mr. Smithers to come back and take another look - and

Tracey," Mrs. Dunn reached for her daughter's hand, "don't be too hard on your Dad. He meant it all for the best."

For the best! Tracey looked at her pony's swollen hocks. How could her mother honestly expect her to forgive him that.

Mr. Smithers was soon back in the stable. "Now let's see what we can do for you, little lady," he murmured to Melody as he set down his equipment. Tracey was surprised to see how the mare regarded him with trust. Her instincts told her none of this had been intended. It had been an accident. She sensed they all wanted to help her over it as easily and painlessly as possible.

Tracey's mouth was dry. If Melody was prepared to forgive . . . she turned to the vet. "Is my father around, Mr. Smithers? I'd like him to be part of Melody's recovery too," she said.

Happy-Go-Unlucky

"Steady, steady ..." Felicity's hands tightened on the reins. Her heels brushed lightly against the skewbald pony's sides. Splash held his head high, one chestnut ear listening to her voice whilst the other, which was white, was intent on the row of bending poles.

Dawn glanced across. "Okay?" she asked and Felicity nodded.

"Three ... two ... one ... go!"

Splash bounced on the spot then leapt away into canter, weaving neatly between the bamboo sticks. By the fourth stick he and Felicity were a clear length ahead of Dawn and Champagne. Felicity pushed her heels down and pulled hard on the right rein. Splash braked hard, feet slithering as he changed direction but going so fast he had to turn a full circle. Champagne, who was a dab hand at on-a-sixpence turns, streaked ahead and got back first.

"I've told you before," Dawn advised as she patted her dun pony's neck. "You ought to do lots of serpentines to get Splash more supple."

Felicity shrugged. "Schooling is so boring!" she grinned. "We'll be all right on the day. Splash knows when it's the real thing and he's saving himself."

Dawn shook her head. "You are impossible – do you want another go?"

"No, they'll turn sour if we do it too often," said Felicity. "How about setting up a handy pony course then?" persisted Dawn.

Felicity agreed, but was not very

Splash braked hard as he changed direction

keen. Setting up a handy pony course involved hulking half-a-dozen straw bales out of the barn, scrounging buckets and wheeling to the paddock a huge tractor tyre from the back of the garage.

Dawn and Champagne went round the course first, slow but faultless. Splash watched, twitching and stamping his feet. The minute Felicity slackened her hold he was away, flying over the jumps only to stop dead in front of the tyre. Felicity crawled down his neck and dismounted to lead him over – two strides in and out of the tyre. Splash sidled and scowled, then followed her. Back on board, they turned for home and flew at the last jump of bales wrapped in old fertiliser sacks. Splash took off too far back and made an enormous leap to get over it. Felicity landed round his ears and when he swerved in surprise she tumbled gracelessly over his shoulder to land on all fours.

Dawn was in stitches. "You should

oin the circus!" she shrieked. "How
many times is it now?"

"I've lost count," Felicity replied as
she got to her feet unhurt. She had
fallen off so many times that she had
learned to land easily. It wasn't so
much that she was a bad rider, but that

Splash was rather unpredictable and
she did take more risks than her friend.
After all, she always thought, that was
part of riding. Felicity glanced at
Dawn and shook her head, smiling to
herself. It was hardly surprising Dawn

never fell off because she rarely proceeded faster than canter ever when she was competing.

Splash was waiting by the gate, an indication that he was bored and wanted to do something else. "How about a ride through the woods?" Felicity suggested.

"Sure, but you'd better help me clean this lot first," agreed Dawn.

They rode back through the leafy woods, popping over fallen logs and then the two friends parted by the main crossroads. Felicity waved her friend goodbye and put Splash into a gallop to race along the wide verge with the wind singing in her ears as he leapt the drainage ditches. "What would I do without you, Splash?" Felicity said, patting her pony's warm neck. "You're always so eager and full of fun, aren't you."

The field Felicity rented was a mile along the road from her family's small terraced house. As always, she took Splash to the yard behind their

house, left the saddle there and then rode up the lane bareback. Once loose, Splash had his own routine to go through – first a roll, then a shake, next he would nudge her for a carrot-end or some mints. Finally he would trot off, shaking his head until he got to the long grass by the stream where he would settle to a drink and some serious grazing.

Monday morning dawned and Felicity was halfway out of bed before she remembered it was half-term. What a luxury it was to remain in bed and plan the day's ride instead. Long live the holidays! Dawn and she had decided to alternate practising with long hacks. Felicity fancied a ride down to the beach in the afternoon and a long gallop at the edge of the sea.

Splash raised his head and stared at Felicity for a full minute before cantering crabwise to the gate, his tail flicking to one side as he shook his head in annoyance.

"What is it then?" she asked. "Come on, stand still!" Felicity slipped the halter over his ears and tied him to the gate before going round to inspect his back feet. She soon found the reason for his strange behaviour. A strand of rusty barbed wire, about eighteen inches long, had got tangled in his tail. "It's Mr. Thruxton we've got to thank for that, isn't it!" Felicity said to Splash as she unwound the wire. The farmer she rented the field from had promised to fix the fence down by the stream when she first turned Splash

out six months ago. Obviously he was no nearer to doing it. Grumbling to herself about negligent farmers, Felicity wound the wire into a little ball and pushed it into the bottom of the hedge out of harm's way. There were a couple of scratches around Splash's pasterns and although they had broken the skin Felicity decided they were nothing to worry about. "Just as well you didn't take it into your head to roll," she told him as she swung on his back. Unconcerned, Splash pulled at some young hawthorn shoots in the hedge.

Dawn was waiting for Felicity in the yard. She reached into her pocket and produced a small packet which she held out. "They were doing a special offer on wormers at the saddlers so I bought ten at once," she announced. "I thought you could probably use one. Splash will take granules, won't he?"

"I don't really know," confessed Felicity.

"What do you usually use then, a syringe?" asked Dawn. "They are so fiddly."

Felicity's cheeks reddened. "I can't remember, I think it was a powder." She had only wormed Splash once, using the packet his previous owner had left amongst his grooming kit.

"Felicity, you are awful!" announced Dawn. "What if he was ill?"

"He's not ill," snapped Felicity. "Don't exaggerate!" Just then, as if to prove her point, Splash struck up an Arab stallion pose and blew through his nostrils like a blood horse. However, Dawn was not to be put off. "Worms could be doing all kinds of hidden damage, eating into his liver and sucking his blood," she said.

"Vampire stories at this time of day? Really Dawn!" Felicity's mother handed the girls ginger biscuits.

"I was just telling Felicity that she ought to worm Splash more often," said Dawn defensively.

"And I was just saying that Splash is in perfect health," Felicity countered.

Mrs. Grant took the packet of powder Dawn had handed over. "It won't hurt to take the precaution," she advised. "Remember that you are responsible for that animal, Felicity. If anything happens to him you will be to blame."

Felicity looked skyward. "Honestly, you two!" she exploded.

Splash finally got his wormer just to pacify everyone, but it did not appear to agree with him. Two days after she gave him the powder, Felicity found her pony behaving very out of sorts. Her mother said it must be a side-effect of the chemicals, but that didn't explain the delay. To cheer him up, she rode over to Dawn's and suggested a gymkhana practice hoping his competitive nature would overcome his mood. At first, he did seem to pick up but soon his head began to droop and he started to drag his feet. Dawn won every race. She patted the dun's neck and congratulated him enthusiastically. Splash on the other hand, was damp with sweat and there were patches of

She patted the dun's neck enthusiastically

foam on his neck where the reins had rubbed. "I think I'll take him back," Felicity said. "He's tired out."

Dawn frowned and said: "That's not like Splash – maybe he's picked up a chill."

Felicity nodded. Did ponies catch chills in the summer? She wasn't sure. All the long walk home Felicity tried to work out what could be wrong with her pony. It certainly wasn't laminitis because there wasn't that much grass in the field. He wasn't coughing and in fact he looked fine. He just wasn't his usual bouncy self. Felicity decided to turn the pony out and give him a few day's rest for that was what doctors always seemed to prescribe for humans feeling under the weather.

The following morning Felicity took Splash's feed up to the field early and was surprised to see him standing at the far end with his head down and his ears drooping. "Splash! Hey, there!" Her call from the gate brought no answering whinny. She rattled the

Suddenly scared, she dropped the bucket

feed bucket. Splash lifted his head but did not move. A lump came into Felicity's throat. Suddenly scared, she dropped the bucket and ran across the rough grass. Splash took three stiff steps towards her and buried his head beneath her arm, letting out a low moan. Tears flooded Felicity's eyes. "Splash! What's happened?" He looked up, his dark eyes filled with pain and confusion. Whatever was wrong, this was no chill!

"Felicity!" Mrs. Grant exclaimed as her daughter ran into the house in muddy wellingtons. "Something's wrong with Splash," Felicity panted dropping down in front of the telephone. Her fingers shook so much she kept missing the page. "Veterinary surgeons ... Davidson ... Farley ... Harcourt! That's the one." Felicity dialled the number, then waited with fingers crossed, listening to the blood pound round her head. She was lucky. Mr. Harcourt was already at one of the farms in the village. The receptionist

said he'd be round in half-an-hour.

"Now then, old son, what's up with you?" Splash succeeded in rolling an eye suspiciously at the sound of this new voice, but did not budge. Mr. Harcourt took the pony's temperature and pulse rate, ran his hands down Splash's legs and then asked Felicity to walk him in a circle. The vet rubbed his chin thoughtfully. "When was his last tetanus innoculation?" he asked.

A flush came up on Felicity's cheeks then drained away to leave them pale and cold. "I don't know," she admitted. "I've only had him six months."

"Well, let's hope there's enough of it left for a booster to do the trick," said Mr. Harcourt as he bent down to take a syringe out of his bag. Splash caught the scent of disinfectant and backed away. Mr. Harcourt smiled. "If he can still pull a face at an injection, he stands a good chance of recovering – there's plenty of fight left in him."

When the vet had gone, Felicity went back home and started clearing one of the outbuildings for use as a stable while Splash was ill. Dawn came round with a couple of bales of hay and straw from her father, while Mrs. Grant brought out a bag of carrots and apples to tempt Splash to eat. Then, there was nothing to do but wait. Poor Splash! When Felicity looked at him she felt nothing but shame. If only she had been more careful. If she had just bothered to find out about those innoculations and got him a proper course of protection from the start, none of this

There was nothing to do but wait and hope!

would be happening. Felicity stayed with Splash all day long, rubbing his forehead and talking to him. Having the will to get better was supposed to make all the difference. He must recover!

Tears burned Felicity's eyes. "I'd never forgive myself if you died, Splash," she told the pony as she stroked his soft neck. "I promise I'll never be so thoughtless again."

Velvet lips nibbled at Felicity's pocket and all at once she felt a surge of hope. As long as he showed an interest in living, she knew that soon he would be well again.